Disney·PIXAR

TOY STORY

Disney·PIXAR

NEMO
FINDING

Disney·PIXAR

a bug's life

Disney·PIXAR

MONSTERS, INC.

Disney·PIXAR
CD Storybook

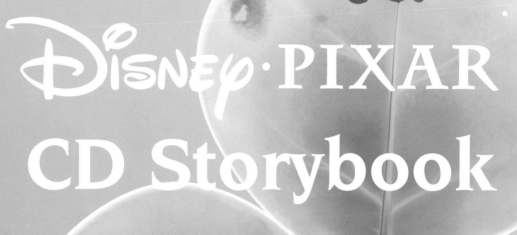

Disney·PIXAR
CD Storybook

Finding Nemo
Monsters, Inc.
A Bug's Life
Toy Story

HINKLER
BOOKS

Hinkler Books Pty Ltd 2004
17-23 Redwood Drive
Dingley, VIC, 3172
www.hinklerbooks.com
Reprinted 2004 (twice)

ISBN: 1 8651 5517 9

Printed and manufactured in China.

Disney·PIXAR CD Storybook

Contents

Little Nemo

Little Nemo had much to prove to his dad.
But then he was caught and his father was sad.
Marlin and Dory searched all through the sea…
Where oh where could my little Nemo be?

He was taken to Sydney, to a dentist's fish tank,
Where right from the start little Nemo's heart sank.
But then he was helped out with all of his troubles
By his new fishy friends: Gill, Bloat, and Bubbles.

The Tank Gang helped Nemo escape down the sink.
But where was his dad? Nemo still had to think.
Then he was found by the forgetful fish, Dory.
Who took him to Marlin, and the end of our story!

Shark Bait

There once was a big shark called Bruce.
Who thought eating meat was no use.
So he stopped eating fish…
His prior favorite dish.
Now, with all fishes, Bruce calls a truce!

FINDING NEMO

At the edge of the Great Barrier Reef in Australia, a brood of clownfish was getting ready to hatch. Marlin and Coral, their father and mother, proudly watched over their eggs in the grotto.

"We still have to name them," Coral said. "I like Nemo."

Suddenly, a barracuda appeared. Marlin rushed to protect Coral, but the barracuda's tail knocked him out cold.

Marlin awoke to an eerie silence. When he swam to the grotto, he found only one tiny egg—injured but still OK.

"There, there, there. It's OK. Daddy's here," Marlin said softly, cradling the egg in his fin. "I promise I will never let anything happen to you . . . Nemo," he whispered to the egg.

From that day on, Marlin was very protective of his son—especially since Nemo was born with a "lucky" fin. It was smaller than his other fin and made him an awkward swimmer. When it was time for Nemo to start school, Marlin didn't want to let his son go.

But Nemo couldn't wait!

"Dad, how old are sea turtles?" Nemo asked on the way to school.

"Well, if I ever meet a sea turtle, I'll ask him," Marlin said.

At school, Nemo climbed on the back of the teacher, Mr. Ray.

To his horror, Marlin learned that Mr. Ray was taking the class on a trip to the Drop-off—it was far too dangerous for Nemo!

The class left the schoolyard later that morning with Mr. Ray and arrived near the Drop-off where they could explore. "Come on, Nemo!" Nemo's new friends sneaked away from the rest of the class. At the edge of the Drop-off, they dared one another to swim up and touch a boat anchored nearby.

"How far can you go?" Tad, one of Nemo's classmates, said to the clownfish.

Just then, Marlin swam over. "Nemo! No!" he cried.

"Dad, I wasn't gonna go–" Nemo said, starting to explain.

"You think you can do these things, but you just can't!" his father said angrily.

"I hate you," Nemo whispered. He felt ashamed and humiliated in front of his classmates.

Mr. Ray heard the commotion and swam over to help. While Marlin was busy talking to the teacher, Nemo swam to the boat and touched it with his fin. He was tired of his dad thinking he was too little and too weak to do anything.

When Marlin heard Nemo's classmates shouting, he looked out toward the boat. "Nemo!" he cried as a diver swam up right behind his son.

"Swim, Nemo, swim!" the kids called.

"Daddy! Help me!" Nemo cried as the diver scooped him up.

But before Marlin could do anything, the diver—and Nemo—were already on the boat. There was no way Marlin could catch up!

Marlin swam to a busy underwater passage. "Has anybody seen a boat? They took my son!" he cried.

Finally, a regal blue tang fish named Dory told him she had seen a boat. "Follow me!" she said.

But Dory had a problem: she couldn't remember anything for more than a few minutes. When she turned and saw Marlin, she got angry with him. "Stop following me, OK?" she exclaimed.

Suddenly, a big shark named Bruce showed up.

Bruce took Dory and Marlin to a sunken submarine. Inside was a meeting of sharks who claimed to be vegetarians. Marlin didn't trust them.

But then Marlin spotted a diving mask—just like the one worn by the diver who had captured Nemo! "What do these markings mean?" he wondered aloud. "I don't read human."

Suddenly, Bruce was overcome with hunger when the mask hit Dory in the nose and caused it to bleed. Once Bruce smelled the blood, he forgot all about being a vegetarian. He chased Dory and Marlin through the submarine, snapping his jaws. The pair raced into a tube that held a torpedo. Marlin and Dory lodged the torpedo in Bruce's mouth to escape. The shark spat it out and seconds later, it exploded!

Far away, a giant hand dropped Nemo into unfamiliar waters. Several friendly but strange fish surrounded him. Bubbles, Peach, Jacques, Bloat, Deb, and Gurgle introduced themselves. Nemo was in a fish tank in a dentist's office! The other fish were thrilled to meet Nemo—a fish from the open sea!

Nigel, a pelican, flew to the window to say hello to his tank friends. The dentist, Dr. Sherman, shooed him away, knocking over a framed picture. Then, Nemo learned his fate: the little clownfish was going to be given to Darla, Dr. Sherman's niece . . . who had shaken her last fish to death!

Then Nemo met the leader of the tank, Gill. Nemo noticed that Gill had a damaged fin, too, and felt a special bond with his new friend.

That night, the tank fish held a ceremony to accept Nemo into their group.

Gill nicknamed Nemo "Shark Bait" and shared his plan for how they would all escape from the tank—a plan that depended on little Nemo!

Meanwhile, Marlin woke after the torpedo's explosion. He and Dory were right on the edge of a deep trench. To make matters worse, Dory accidentally dropped the diver's mask!

As they swam down after the mask to darker waters, a glowing orb appeared. It was attached to a hungry anglerfish! While Marlin struggled with the fierce angler, Dory used the fish's light to see the writing on the mask. "P. Sherman, 42 Wallaby Way, Sydney," she read.

After they escaped from the anglerfish, Dory asked a school of moonfish to give her directions to Sydney. Marlin had already started swimming away when one of the moonfish gave Dory a tip. "When you come to a trench, swim through it, not over it," he warned her.

Soon Marlin and Dory reached the trench. But instead of swimming through it as Dory had suggested, Marlin convinced her to swim over it. They were instantly surrounded by a forest of jellyfish. How would they ever escape?

When Marlin realized the tops of the jellyfish didn't sting, he came up with a plan. He spoke about a game in which whoever can hop the fastest out of these jellyfish wins. He warned Dory not to touch the tentacles—only the tops

Dory had almost made it through when she got stung. Marlin pulled her free, but not before he was stung, too.

Back in the fish tank, Gill gave Nemo swimming lessons while the two swapped stories.

Gill caught Nemo looking at his biggest scar. "My first escape—landed on dental tools," Gill told him. "I was aiming for the toilet. All drains lead to the ocean, kid."

Later, the fish began the first step of their escape plan: get the tank dirty. If they could break the filter, Dr. Sherman would have to clean the tank—and that would mean removing the fish and putting them in plastic bags. While the bags were on the counter, the fish would roll themselves out the window to freedom.

Coached by Gill, Nemo swam into the filter and wedged a pebble in the rotating fan.

But the pebble came loose and Nemo was sucked toward the sharp blades. The other fish rescued him, but Nemo was terrified.

The escape plan was ruined—and Gill realized he had put Nemo in danger.

Meanwhile, some sea turtles had rescued Marlin and Dory after their dangerous encounter with the jellyfish. "Takin' on the jellies–awesome!" Crush, a surfer turtle, proclaimed.

Marlin told the younger turtles the story of his quest to find his son. Soon the tale was being passed throughout the ocean from sea creature to sea creature, until Nigel overheard the news from another pelican.

Nigel flew back to the dentist's office to tell Nemo that Marlin was on his way. Inspired by his father's bravery, Nemo grabbed a pebble and rushed over to the filter. He successfully jammed it into the fan.

"Shark Bait, you did it!" the Tank Gang cheered. Now that the filter was broken, would the tank get dirty enough to need a cleaning before Dr. Sherman's niece arrived?

Out in the ocean, Marlin and Dory bid the sea turtles good-bye. Marlin called, "Crush! How old are you?" He couldn't wait to tell Nemo the answer when he saw him.

Marlin and Dory swam and swam until they were lost. Dory asked a blue whale for directions, but they were sucked into its humongous mouth.

Just when it looked like things couldn't get any worse, the water inside the whale's mouth began to drain into its stomach!

In Sydney Harbor, a blue whale surfaced and spouted. Riding atop the spray were Marlin and Dory!

"Dory! We made it!" Marlin cried joyfully. "We're going to find my son! All we have to do is find the boat that took him." The problem was, there were boats as far as the eye could see.

Back in the tank, Nemo and his friends felt their luck was changing for the better. Without a working filter, the tank was a nice, slimy green.

Dr. Sherman swiped his finger across the inside of the glass. "Crikey!" he said with disgust. "I'd better clean the fish tank before Darla gets here."

The Tank Gang rejoiced.

"Are you ready to see your dad, kid?" Gill asked Nemo.

"Uh-huh!" Nemo cried happily.

The next morning when the fish woke up, the water was perfectly clear. The tank had already been cleaned by a brand-new, high-tech filter called the Aqua Scum 2003! The dentist would never have to clean the tank again.

"Boss must have installed it last night while we were sleeping," guessed Gill. The fish realized that their escape plan was ruined again.

"Wh–what are we gonna do?" Nemo asked, panicking.

Marlin and Dory had searched all night for the boat that took Nemo to no avail. Then, suddenly, a pelican swooped down and scooped them up.

The pelican landed on the dock, threw its head back, and prepared to enjoy its catch. "I didn't come this far to be breakfast!" Marlin cried. He and Dory stubbornly wedged themselves sideways in the bird's throat.

Nigel, perched nearby, watched as the choking pelican stumbled around the dock. Nigel raced over and whacked him on the back.

Marlin and Dory flew out of the pelican's mouth. As he flopped helplessly on the dock, Marlin said with a gasp, "I've got to find my son, Nemo!"

Nigel couldn't believe it. "He's that fish that's been fighting the whole ocean!" he exclaimed, looking at Marlin.

By this time, a flock of hungry seagulls had gathered. "Mine! Mine! Mine!" they shouted.

"Hop inside my mouth if you want to live," whispered Nigel.

Marlin and Dory jumped inside Nigel's beak, and they were off. The seagulls followed, but Nigel's tricky maneuvers led the birds smack into a boat's sail.

Back at the dentist's office, Dr. Sherman stuck a net into the tank and captured Nemo. "Jump in and swim down!" Gill yelled. The rest of the Tank Gang joined Nemo in the net and forced it away from the dentist.

But suddenly, Dr. Sherman scooped Nemo into a plastic bag. Then he set the plastic bag by the tank.

"Roll, kid, roll!" the others cried. Nemo swam furiously back and forth. But the dentist spotted the wobbly bag and stuck it in a tray to keep Nemo from falling. Nemo and his friends were worried. Darla would be arriving any minute!

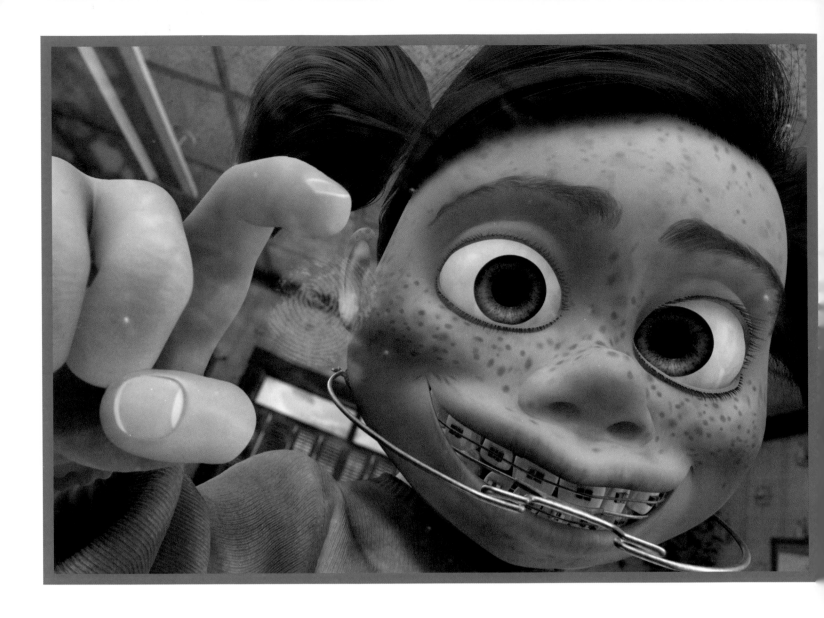

Suddenly, a bell rang! Darla burst into the room. "Fishy! Fishy! Fishy!" the dentist's niece cried.

Dr. Sherman reached for the bag. Inside, Nemo was floating upside down–playing dead! Everyone in the tank cheered. If the dentist flushed Nemo down the toilet, he'd travel through the plumbing to freedom! But their joy instantly turned to horror when Dr. Sherman started walking Nemo over to the trashcan instead!

Just then, Nigel showed up on the window ledge and flew inside. The dentist dropped Nemo's bag onto the dental tray. Nemo spotted Darla and again played dead.

At that moment, Marlin peeked out of Nigel's mouth–and saw Nemo floating upside down. He feared the worst.

Dr. Sherman pushed Nigel back outside and shut the window.

Darla picked up Nemo's bag and shook it. Gill knew he had to do something. The other tank fish launched Gill out of the tank, and he landed right on Darla's head!

Nemo's bag popped and he fell onto a dental mirror on the tray. Gill flipped himself from Darla's head onto the tray. "Tell your dad I said hi," Gill said—and then he smacked his tail on the dental mirror, causing Nemo to fly over Darla's head and into the spit sink. Nemo escaped down the drain!

Back in the harbor, Nigel dropped Marlin and Dory into the sea. Overcome with sadness, Marlin said good-bye to Dory. She pleaded to stay with him—he had become like family to her.

But it was no use. Marlin couldn't stand to be around any reminder of his failed search for his son. He swam off and began his long journey home.

Meanwhile, Nemo rode the rapids through the water treatment plant. When he finally popped out of a pipe in the harbor, he was greeted by two hungry crabs. Nemo quickly swam away to avoid their snapping claws and had just missed his dad passing by.

Escaping from the crabs, Nemo swam back toward the harbor and went off in search of his father. But instead, he found Dory swimming in circles and sobbing.

Dory and Nemo introduced themselves to each other—but of course Dory had no memory of Nemo or the search she had been on to find him. Nevertheless, the two swam off together.

Luckily, Dory spotted the word "Sydney" on the water treatment pipe—and suddenly remembered everything. She led Nemo back to where she had last seen Marlin.

Dory described Nemo's dad and asked the crabs if they had seen him. They wouldn't talk—until she threatened to turn them into seagull food!

"All right, I'll talk," one of the crabs cried. "He went to the fishing grounds!"

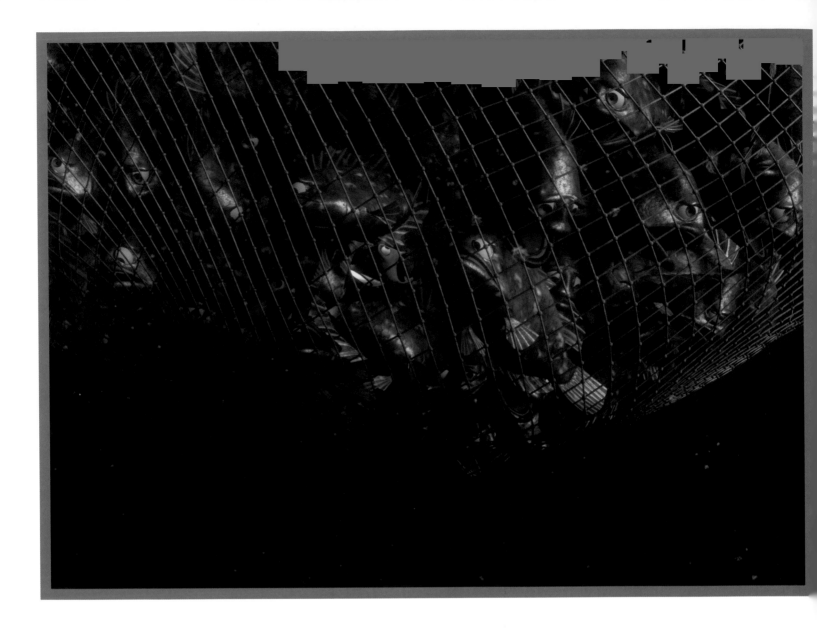

Dory and Nemo were reunited with Marlin in the fishing grounds nearby. Before they had a chance to celebrate, an enormous net swept up Dory along with a huge school of groupers.

Thinking quickly, Nemo said, "Let's tell every fish to swim down!" Nemo swam inside the net to help.

"No, Nemo . . ." Marlin cried, and then stopped. He didn't want to let Nemo go—but he then realized that Nemo could do it.

"Swim down!" Marlin cried—and soon all the fish had broken through the net. But where was Nemo?

Dory and Marlin found him beneath the net. Marlin was relieved when Nemo's eyes fluttered open. "Dad, I'm sorry. I don't hate you," Nemo said.

"Oh, thank goodness!" Marlin cried. "And guess what? I met a sea turtle. They live to be a hundred and fifty years old!"

Weeks later, Marlin and Nemo raced to school. They had some amazing tales to tell–but most of their friends didn't believe them. Then, Bruce and the other sharks showed up with Dory. Everyone's mouths hung open as the giant sharks greeted Marlin.

Nemo swam onto Mr. Ray's back and the class started to leave. "Oh, wait! I forgot something," Nemo said.

Nemo swam back to his dad and gave him a big hug. "Love ya, Dad," said Nemo.

"I love you, too, son," said Marlin. "Now go have an adventure."

Monsters Monsters

Monsters, monsters, everywhere,
Their mission is to give children a scare.
Hiding in closets in the deep, dark night
Then jumping out quickly to give kids a fright.
But monsters are not really as mean as they seem.
They just need volts for their city, it's powered by scream
In fact monsters are really more scared of you,
Just sneak up behind them and then cry out "Boo!"

Monsters Alive

One, two, three, four, five,
I caught a monster alive.
Six, seven, eight, nine, ten,
Then I let it go again.
Why did I let it go?
Because it scared my sister, Jo.
But why did she get a fright?
Because he jumped out in the night!

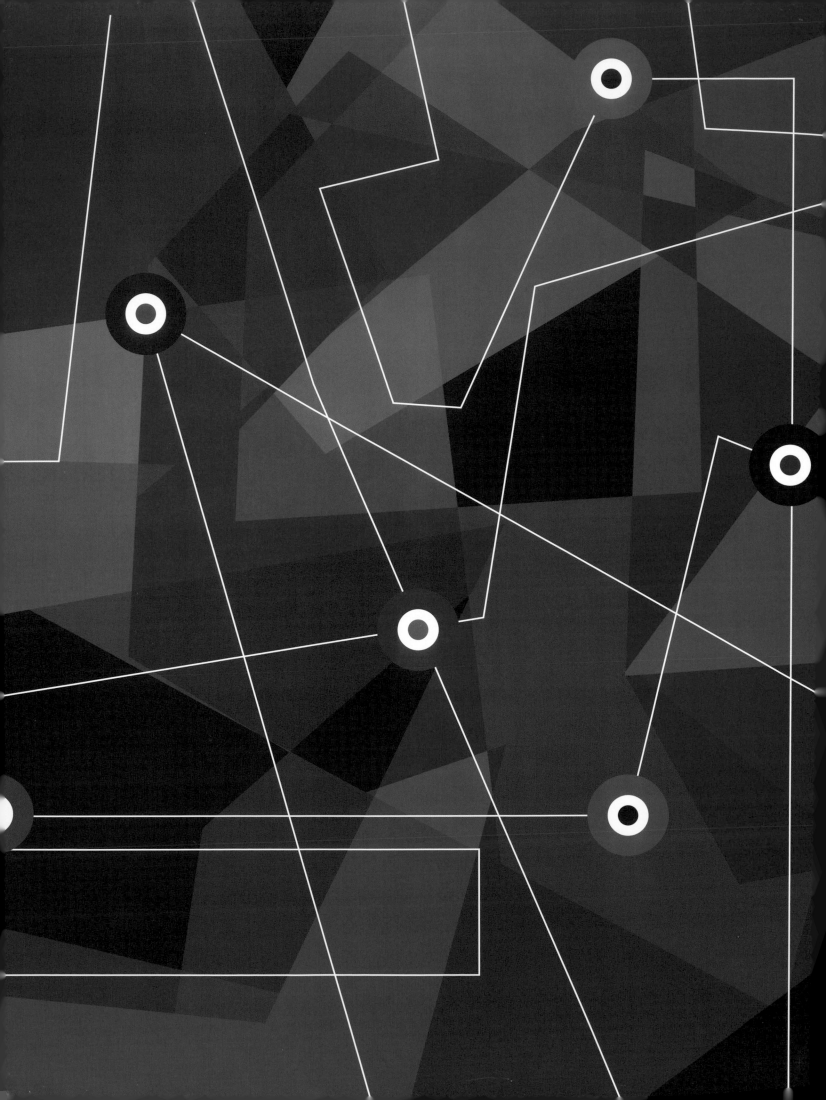

DISNEY·PIXAR

MONSTERS, INC.

In the dark bedroom of a little boy, the closet door creaked open.

The boy snapped awake as a huge, scary monster crept up to his bed and spread its arms wide, preparing to roar! But the boy's scream scared the monster and it staggered back and fell to the floor.

Suddenly, the lights came on and the bedroom wall opened up.

The boy turned out to be just a robot and the monster, known as Bile, was a trainee. He was learning to scare children at Monsters, Inc., the largest scream-processing factory in Monstropolis. Ms. Flint, the scare instructor, turned to the class of trainees.

"Can anyone tell me Mr. Bile's big mistake?"

No-one answered.

"Mr. Bile left the closet door open," said Ms. Flint. "And leaving the door open is the worst mistake any employee can make because..."

"It could let in a child!"

The trainees spun around to see Mr. Waternoose, the crab-like, five-eyed president of Monsters, Inc., at the back of the room.

"There's nothing more toxic or deadly than a human child. A single touch could kill you!" he declared.

Meanwhile, the company's best Scarer, a huge, hairy, blue-spotted monster named James P. Sullivan, or Sulley for short, was walking to work with his friend, Mike Wazowski. Mike was a little green ball of a monster with one enormous eye. Mike wanted to drive his new car, but Sulley disagreed. "Mikey, there's a scream shortage."

You see, monsters captured the screams of children and used them to power Monstropolis, but kids weren't as easy to scare as they used to be.

Mike and Sulley arrived at the factory for work. It was a big day for Sulley because he was about to break the all-time scare record. They crossed the lobby to the receptionist, Celia, who was also Mike's girlfriend. "Oh, Shmoopsie-Poo..."

"Googley bear!" she replied.

It was Celia's birthday, and Mike was taking her to a fancy sushi restaurant that night to celebrate. "I will see you at quittin' time and not a minute later," he said.

"Okay, sweetheart."

Sulley and Mike crossed to their work station on the Scare Floor, the busy place where all the scaring in the factory occurred.

Mike slipped a card key into a slot and a door emerged from a huge overhead vault and dropped into place in front of them. At the next station, a lizard-like monster named Randall made his preparations.

Randall was the company's second-best Scarer, but he was determined to take the lead. Sulley waved to him, "Hey–may the best monster win."

"I plan to," was Randall's reply.

Red lights lit up above all the doors to show they were active.

Mike cheered Sulley on as he opened his door and crossed into a child's room.

"You're the boss, you're the boss, you're the big hairy boss!"

Sullivan kept his lead over Randall. "Oh, I'm feeling good today, Mikey!"

"'Atta boy, 'atta boy! Another door coming right up."

Randall's assistant, Fungus, turned to his boss. "You're still behind, Randall."

"Just get me another door!" Randall yelled.

Suddenly an alarm sounded. "2319! We have a 2319!" Another monster, George, had come out of his door with a human sock stuck to his back. "Get it off! Get it off!"

Agents from the Child Detection Agency, or CDA, swarmed onto the Scare Floor. They knocked poor George to the ground, picked off the sock, and blew it up. George was disinfected in a shower and shaved clean.

Mr. Waternoose was not pleased. "An entire Scare Floor out of commission. What else can go wrong?"

Despite the temporary setback, Sulley still had a good day. "Another day like this and that scare record's in the bag!"

Mike headed out quickly.

"Oooh, the love boat is about to set sail."

Just then, Roz, the slug-like dispatcher, stopped him. "Hello, Wazowski. I'm sure you filed your paperwork correctly. For once."

Mike was caught. He hadn't filed it, and Celia was waiting. But Sulley jumped in and offered to file the paperwork for him.

"On my desk, Sulley!" said Mike.

When Sulley returned to the empty Scare Floor he discovered a lone door that had accidentally been left behind. The door's red light was on. Sulley peered into the child's bedroom. No monsters there.

But then he turned around to find a little girl holding his tail!

Quickly he put the girl back in her room and took off. In the locker room he found that the girl was still clinging to his back! "Kitty!" the girl said.

Sulley scooped the girl into a duffel bag and ran back to the Scare Floor. But Randall was there sending the girl's door back to the vault. Sulley couldn't get her back to her room.

Sulley took the duffel bag and rushed to the crowded restaurant where Mike and Celia were dining. "Get out of here, you're ruining everything," Mike said to Sulley.

"Look in the bag!" Sulley pleaded.

Mike looked, but it was too late. The kid was out of the bag. "Boo!"

"Ahhh! A kid!"

Panicked diners fled the restaurant as CDA agents arrived. Mike and Sulley snatched up the kid and ran. Mike looked back but the CDA was already taking Celia away. "Michael? Michael!"

"Well, I don't think that date could've gone any worse," Mike said with a sigh.

The terrified monsters took the girl back to their apartment. She ran around happily until she grabbed a one-eyed teddy bear and Mike objected. "Hey, hey, that's it. No-one touches little Mikey!" And he grabbed the teddy back.

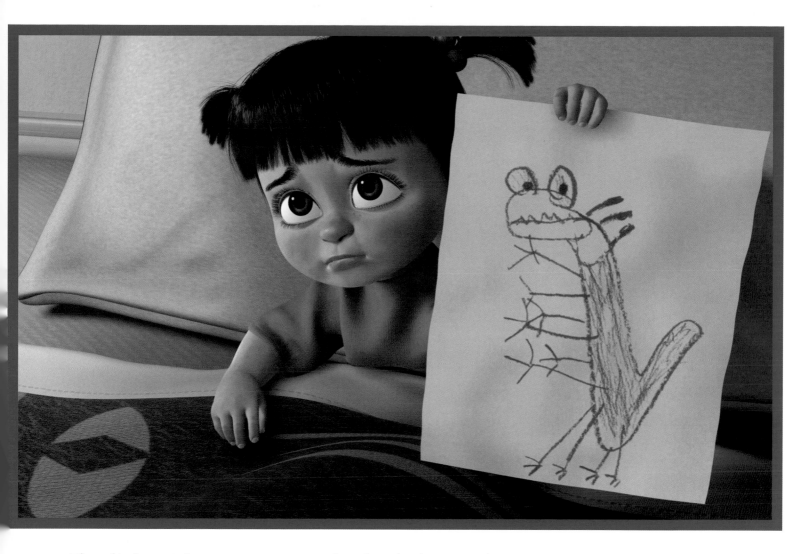

The little girl's scream made the lights in the apartment surge brightly. Panicked, Mike ran to the window and pulled the blinds shut. But as he tried to get the bear back to the girl, he slipped, flew through the air, and landed in a wastebasket. Amazingly, her laughter caused all the lights in the whole building to light up and blow out.

"What was that?" asked Mike.

"I have no idea, but it would be really great if it didn't do it again."

After a lot of playing, the little girl finally got tired, and Sulley put her to bed in his room. But as Sulley started to leave, she whimpered and pointed to the closet. She showed Sulley a picture she had drawn.

"Hey, that looks like Randall. Randall's your monster," Sulley said. "How 'bout I sit here until you fall asleep?" Sulley comforted her gently until she fell asleep. Then he returned to the living room. "Hey, Mike – this might sound crazy, but I don't think that kid's dangerous."

Sulley figured the best plan was to get the girl back to her room through her closet door at Monsters, Inc. The next day he disguised her in a little monster costume and took her back to the factory.

"Sulley, a mop, a couple of lights, and some chair fabric are not gonna fool anyone. Loch Ness, Big Foot, the Abominable Snowman. They all got one thing in common, pal . . . banishment! We could be next!" Of course, they promptly ran into Mr. Waternoose.

"Boo!" the disguised little girl said.

"Ah ha! James!" said Mr. Waternoose. "Is this one yours?"

"Uh, actually . . . that's my . . . uh, cousin's . . . sister's . . . uh, daughter, sir," Sulley replied.

The guys ducked into the restroom with the girl and she and Sulley played hide and seek. "Where did she go? Did she turn invisible?"

"Boo!" But someone was coming. The girl acted scared and all three hid in a stall just before Randall and Fungus entered.

"What are we going to do about the child?" said Fungus.

"Shhh! You just get the machine up and running, I'll take care of the kid," said Randall. "And when I find whoever let it out . . . they're dead!"

Mike and Sulley hurried the girl to their station on the Scare Floor. Mike swiped a card key and brought a door down from the vault.

"Mike, that's not her door. Her door was white. And it had flowers on it. This isn't Boo's door."

"Boo? What's Boo? Sulley, you're not supposed to name it! Once you name it, you start getting attached to it! Now say good-bye to—Where'd it go? What'd you do with it?"

Sulley scanned the floor for her. "Where is she? Aah! Boo!"

He took off looking for her. Mike tried to stop him.

"Somebody else will find the kid, it'll be their problem, not ours!"

Mike passed Randall in the hall just as Celia approached.

"Michael Wazowski! Last night was one of the worst nights of my entire life bar none!"

"I thought you liked sushi," Mike said.

"Sushi?! You think this is about sushi?!"

Randall's ears pricked up. He knew that the little girl had been found in a sushi restaurant and he guessed that Mike was involved.

"Where's the kid, Mike?" Randall asked.

"You're not pinning this on me!"

Randall told Mike the Scare Floor was about to empty out for lunch and that Boo's door would be in his station. "You have until then to put the kid back."

Meanwhile, Sulley searched everywhere for Boo. He finally spotted her climbing into a garbage can. "No!"

But CDA agents stopped to get Sulley's autograph just as some workers appeared and wheeled off the can. Sulley ran up in time to see the workers tip the can down the trash chute, not knowing that Boo had already climbed out and toddled off. He raced down to the basement where the trash was processed and watched horrified as it was smashed into a cube by a giant compactor.

Mike caught up to Sulley crying and cradling the garbage cube in his arms. "I can still hear her little voice."

Just then a group of day-care children walked by and Sulley heard Boo. "Kitty!"

"Boo!" The delighted Sulley picked Boo up and hugged her tightly.

"Okay, Sulley. That's enough. Let's go . . ."

On the deserted Scare Floor, Mike spotted Boo's door set up in Randall's station. "There it is! Just like Randall said!"

"Mike, what are you thinking?

We can't trust Randall. He's after Boo."

"You want me to prove everything's on the up and up? Fine." Mike marched into Boo's room and began bouncing on her bed. Suddenly, a large box flew up from behind the bed and trapped him. After a moment, Randall peeked out of Boo's room. Sulley comforted Boo and they hid as Randall loaded the box containing Mike on a cart and rolled it away.

Mr. Waternoose brought Mike and Sulley to an active door.

"Uh, sir, that's not her door," said Mike.

"I know, I know . . . It's yours." And he shoved Mike and Sulley through the door and slammed it shut behind them.

The two friends found themselves in a snowstorm in the Himalayas. "We're in the human world! Oh, what a great idea going to your old pal Waternoose! Too bad he was in on the whole thing!"

Sulley tried desperately to re-open the door, but it was no use. They were stuck. Suddenly, the Yeti, a huge, hairy monster, appeared.

"I understand. It ain't easy being banished."

The Yeti invited the two distressed monsters back to his cave.

The Yeti shared his food, talked about his life and mentioned a village at the bottom of the mountain. As soon as Sulley heard this, he began frantically building a makeshift sled out of the Yeti's belongings. Mike was furious. "What about us?! Ever since that kid came in you've ignored everything I've said and now look where we are. We were about to break the record, Sulley!"

"None of that matters now. Boo's in trouble! I think there might be a way to save her."

Mike was not interested in risking his life to help her, so Sulley grabbed a lantern, hopped on the sled, and sped off down the mountain alone.

Sulley found an active closet door in the village and crossed back into Monsters, Inc. He burst onto the Scare Floor and raced for Randall's secret lab. "Boo!"

Boo was strapped in the chair, the Scream Extractor inches from her face, as Waternoose and Randall looked on. Sulley charged in like a bull and smashed the machine out of Boo's path.

He grabbed Boo and they took off.

"Stop him! Don't let them get away!" said Mr. Waternoose.

Suddenly, Mike showed up and tried to apologize. Sulley just dragged him along, with Randall chasing after them. They ran to the Scare Floor and Sulley grabbed onto a door on its way back to the door vault. Sulley, Mike, and Boo clung to the door as it sailed through the enormous vault on a conveyor belt, surrounded by doors as far as the eye could see. Just then they spotted Randall riding on another door straight toward them.

Sulley shouted. "Make her laugh!"

Mike looked at Boo then socked himself in the head. The red lights above their door and all the doors in the vault lit up. The trio jumped through the door and found themselves in a house on a beautiful Hawaiian beach. "Why couldn't we get banished here?" said Mike.

They quickly ran out of the house, into a neighbor's house, and through another door back into the vault. But Randall was still right behind them. "Hurry up!" Keep moving!"

Randall closed in, seized Boo, and disappeared with her into a door. Knowing Sullivan was not far behind, Randall waited then attacked Sullivan as soon as he appeared in the doorway.

"You've been number one for too long, Sullivan! Now your time is up! And don't worry, I'll take good care of the kid!"

Suddenly Randall's head jerked back. It was Boo, pulling him back! Sulley was saved and was able to get back into the room.

"She's not scared of you anymore. Looks like you're out of a job."

Sulley pushed Randall through a door into a run-down trailer in a swamp. "Mama, 'nother gator got in the house," a boy in the house cried.

"'Nother gator?! Gimme that shovel," his mom yelled.

Just then, Boo's door rode by and they jumped on it. But before they could get it open, it lurched off in another direction.

"What's happening?"

The door sailed back down toward the Scare Floor where Mr. Waternoose was waiting for them, surrounded by CDA agents.

As the door landed, Mike threw one of Boo's socks at the agents and they all panicked. In the commotion, Mike took off carrying Boo's costume and the agents followed him. Sulley grabbed Boo's door, and he and Boo ran the other way. Only Mr. Waternoose saw Sulley had Boo and he chased after them alone.

Sulley ran with Boo to the training room. He quickly put Boo's door in the fake bedroom and hid Boo in the bed to make it look like Boo's room. Mr. Waternoose arrived at the door.

"She's home now. Just leave her alone!"

"I can't do that, she's seen too much! I'll kidnap a thousand children before I let this company die! And I'll silence anyone who gets in my way!"

Suddenly, the lights came on and the walls opened up. Mike was manning the controls, and Waternoose was caught red-handed.

As Mike and Sulley watched, CDA agents crossed onto the stage, arrested him, and led him away.

Sulley used a card key to activate Boo's door. She was delighted to see her room again, and showed Sulley around.

She looked in her closet.

"Nothing's coming out of your closet to scare you anymore. Right? Yeah. Good-bye, Boo."

"Kitty," Boo said sadly.

Sulley quietly stepped into the closet and closed the door behind him. The CDA then shredded Boo's door to prevent future monsters from getting into her room. Sulley could never see Boo again.

Thanks to Sulley's discovery of the superior power of children's laughter, Monsters, Inc. soon switched from screams to giggles. Sulley took over as president and Mike became their best Laugh Collector, keeping kids in stitches. But Sulley was sad. He missed Boo.

One day, Mike surprised him. "Hey Sulley, there's something I want to show you."

It was Boo's reconstructed door, carefully glued back together. Sulley couldn't believe it. He cautiously opened the door.

"Boo?"

"Kitty!"

The Ants go Marching

The ants go marching one by one, hurrah, hurrah,
The ants go marching one by one, hurrah, hurrah,
The ants go marching one by one,
They march all day long in the beating sun,
And they keep on marching,
Collecting piles of food.

The ants go marching two by two, hurrah, hurrah,
The ants go marching two by two, hurrah, hurrah,
The ants go marching two by two,
They're always so busy, so much to do,
And they keep on marching,
Collecting piles of food.

The ants go marching three by three, hurrah, hurrah,
The ants go marching three by three, hurrah, hurrah,
The ants go marching three by three,
One day they stopped and, finally,
They can halt their marching,
To eat their pile of food.

Two Ants in Love

Two ants in love went up the hill
To fetch some food and water.
Atta fell down,
And broke her crown,
And Flik came tumbling after.

It was harvest time, and all the ants were bringing in grain. Princess Atta was in charge because she was training to be the Queen. One day during harvest, a big stalk of grain fell right on top of her.

"I'm sorry, I'm sorry, I'm sorry, I'm sorry, I'm sorry! I'm so sorry, sorry, please forgive me, I'm sorry." It was Flik. He had knocked over the stalk with his latest invention. "This is my new idea for harvesting grain. No more picking individual kernels, you can just cut down the entire stalk!"

Flik was always inventing things, but nobody, including Atta, thought they were any good.

"Please, Flik just go," said Atta wearily.

When Flik trudged back to work, Dot, Atta's younger sister, ran to catch up with him.

"Hey, Flik! Flik, wait up! I like your inventions."

"Really? Well you're the first. I'm beginning to think nothing I do works. I'm never going to make a difference."

"Me neither," said Dot. "I'm a royal ant, and I can't even fly yet. I'm too little."

Flik showed Dot a stone. "Pretend that that's a seed. Now do you see our tree? Everything that made that giant tree is already contained inside this tiny little seed. You might not feel like you can do much now, but that's just because, well, you're not a tree yet. You're still a seed."

Suddenly an alarm went off, and everyone raced for cover. On the way, Flik dropped his invention next to the huge pile of grain he and Dot had been gathering. When he did, he knocked the pile sideways, and all the grain went over the edge of a cliff. "No, no, no, no, no, no, no!" he said.

Just then, the sky got dark, and this awful buzzing started. It was a gang of grasshoppers, led by Hopper who was really, really, mean. That's why the ants were gathering grain. It was an offering to keep Hopper satisfied. And now you might say he was a little upset.

"Where's my food?!" Hopper yelled. Flik hung his head. "It was an accident?"

Hopper got this horrible grin on his face. "Hey, I'm a compassionate insect. There's still a few months till the rains come. So you can all just try again."

The Queen didn't like it. "But Hopper, it's almost the rainy season. We need this time to gather food for ourselves."

"It seems to me that you ants are forgetting your place. So let's double the order of food! You ants have a nice summer. Let's ride!" With a loud roar, Hopper and his gang went buzzing off into the sky.

Later, Flik was brought before the Council, and Atta read the charges. "Flik, you are sentenced to one month digging in the tunnels."

Flik had an idea, as usual. "We could find bigger bugs to come here and fight, and forever rid us of Hopper and his gang. Oh, I-I-I could travel to the City! I could search there!"

Now, Atta and the Council didn't think Flik could really do it. But they figured at least he wouldn't be around to cause trouble. So they agreed. The next morning, Flik packed his things and headed off to the City. There was just one bug who thought he had a chance.

It was Dot. "Bye, Flik! Good luck, Flik!"

Meanwhile, in the City, P.T. Flea's circus was putting on a show.

There was Rosie the insect-taming spider and Dim the rhino beetle. There were the clowns, Slim, Francis, and Heimlich. There were the acrobats, Tuck and Roll, and a magic act, Manny and Gypsy.

But there was also an audience full of rowdy flies.

P.T. Flea tried to save the show by announcing a brand-new stunt, using matches, lighter fluid, and flypaper. "Flaming Death!"

The circus bugs tried it and, well, let's just say it didn't go well and P.T. got burned.

After the show, P.T. dumped the bugs in town. "You're all fired!"

The bugs went into this flimsy, dingy cafe and guess who was there? The flies! They started making fun of Francis, a ladybug who's actually a guy. To hold them off, Francis, Slim and Heimlich went into their Robin Hood act. They pretended to have swords, but Francis was really using Slim and Heimlich was using a toothpick.

"Back to Sherwood Forest! Schnell! Schnell!"

But it didn't work. The doorway was already crowded, so when the circus bugs tried to leave, the whole place tipped over on its side, knocking the flies out cold.

It just so happened that Flik was nearby, looking for help.

He only saw the end of the fight, but that was enough. "You're perfect! I have been scouting for bugs with your exact talents!"

The bugs were thrilled. They thought Flik was a talent scout! And Flik thought he had found warrior bugs.

Back at Ant Island, it was Dot's day to be on lookout. Using Flik's leaf telescope, Dot spotted him coming home with the circus bugs!

"Flik! He did it! He did it!"

Flik brought the bugs to Atta and the Council, hoping to impress them. Plus he was in love with Atta. "So, Princess Atta, w-what do you think?"

"No, no, no. Wait. This was not supposed to happen," said Atta.

Flik was disappointed, but not the circus ladybug, Francis. He and the circus bugs still thought they'd be doing a show. "Ladies and gentlemen, boys and girls of all ages—our troupe here guarantees a performance like no other. Why, when your grasshopper friends get here, we are gonna knock them dead!" All the ants cheered!

To show how happy they were, Dot's class presented a picture showing the circus bugs fighting the grasshoppers. "We drew one of you dying because our teacher said it would be more dramatic," said Dot.

The bugs stared at the picture, and that's when it hit them. They weren't going to put on a show. Flik had hired them to fight!

The circus bugs tried to sneak off, but Flik caught up. "No, no, no, no, no, no! You can't go! I'm desperate!"

Just then, a giant shadow passed over them. It was a bird, and it was hungry!

Flik and the bugs didn't know it, but Dot had been following them.

To get a closer look, Dot climbed to the top of a dandelion puff. It wasn't a great move because she took off into the air and all of a sudden, the bird turned and headed straight towards her! There was just one thing to do—Dot let go!

The bird missed Dot, and she went falling toward the ground. Flik and the circus bugs heard the commotion. Quickly Francis flew over and caught her. "I gotcha! I gotcha!"

He caught Dot in his arms, but the force of it knocked them into a ditch, and a big rock fell on Francis' leg. The bird tried to follow, but the circus bugs lured it away. They had saved Dot's life!

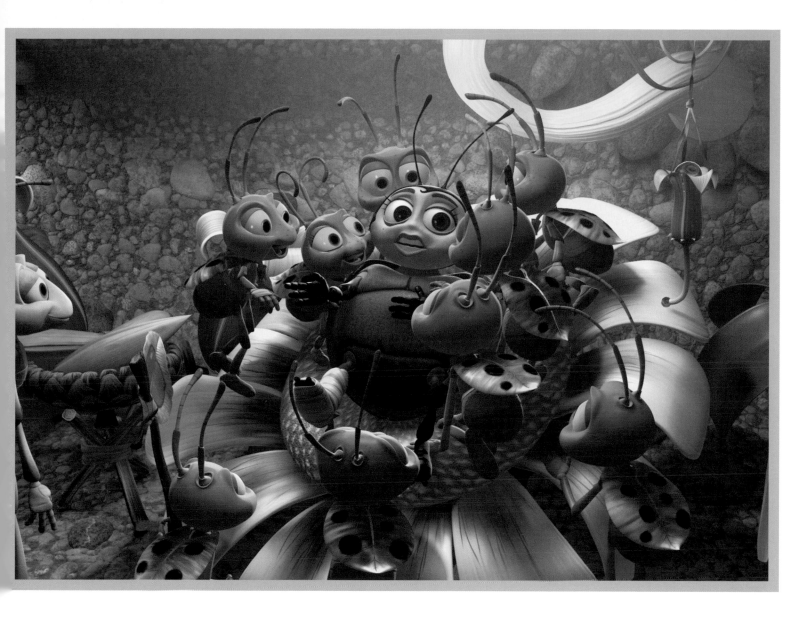

Suddenly the circus bugs were heroes! Later, Dot went with her little ant friends, the Blueberries, to see Francis, who was recovering from his injury.

"We voted you our honorary den mother!" the Blueberries declared.

But it wasn't enough to make the bugs stay. They were circus bugs, not warriors. Then Flik had a great idea. It came to him when he remembered that Hopper was afraid of birds. "Oh! Oh! Oh! This is perfect!"

Flik went running to the circus bugs and told them his plan.

"All right. We are going to build a bird. A bird that we can operate from the inside, which would then be hoisted above our anthill . . ." He convinced the bugs they wouldn't be in any danger. All they had to do was keep pretending they were warriors and tell the Council that they had made up the plan.

The Council loved the idea! Right away, the whole colony started work on the bird, and the circus bugs pitched in. When the bird was finished, they hoisted it up into a tree. Finally, they were ready for the grasshoppers!

Atta looked on proudly. "Would you just look at this colony? I-I don't even recognise them. And I have you bugs to thank for it. So, thank you. And thank you for finding them, Flik."

Flik got all embarrassed. "Me?"

He turned toward Atta, and she leaned down close to him.
Somehow, the two of them got their antennas tangled.
I bet you didn't know that ants could blush!

That night the ants had a huge party. Everyone was having a great time, until the alarm sounded. Atta hurried to the front. "Battle stations, everyone! This is not a drill!"

Someone was coming, all right, but it wasn't the grasshoppers. It was P.T. Flea, and he was looking for the circus bugs!

"Flaming Death is a huge hit! We'll be the top circus act in the business!"

Atta stared at the bugs. "You mean, you're not warriors?"

P.T. laughed. "Are you kidding? These guys are the lousiest circus bugs you've ever seen!"

Thorny, the chief engineer, couldn't believe it. "You mean to tell me that our entire defensive strategy was concocted by clowns?"

Francis tried to help. "Hey, hey, hey, hey! We really thought Flik's idea was going to work. Oops!"

Atta glared at Flik. After all the excitement, the bird had turned out just to be another one of Flik's crazy ideas. Before, Atta had thought she might be falling in love with him, but not now. "Tell me this isn't true."

"But the bird! T-The bird will work! Just—"

"You lied, Flik. You lied to the colony. You lied to me," said Atta angrily. "I want you to leave Flik. And this time, don't come back."

Flik was miserable, and so was Dot. She felt awful watching him leave with the circus bugs. But the ants had work to do gathering food for the grasshoppers. They hauled grain until they were ready to drop, but it wasn't enough. When Hopper came, he was really mad!

"You little termites! I give you a second chance and this is all I get?"

Atta tried to explain. "But Hopper, we ran out of time."

It was no use. Hopper's gang rounded everyone up and herded them back to the fields. "Not one ant sleeps until we get every scrap of food on this island!"

In all the commotion, Dot sneaked away with her friends, the Blueberries. They hid in their clubhouse, where they overheard some grasshoppers discussing their plan. After the ants picked all the food, Hopper was going to squish the Queen!

Dot turned to her friends. "Stay here, I'm gonna get help."

She tried to go after Flik but ran right into Thumper, a scary grasshopper who was more like a vicious dog. He chased Dot to a cliff and forced her over the edge. She fell down . . . down . . . then suddenly she wasn't falling anymore. Her wings had finally sprouted. She was flying!

Later, zipping through the air, Dot caught up with Flik and the circus bugs. When she told Flik they could still use the bird they had built, he just shook his head sadly.

"Forget everything I ever told you, all right. Dot, that bird is a guaranteed failure. Just like me."

Francis and the bugs disagreed. "Kid, say the word and we'll follow you into battle." Flik hung his head and walked away. Dot picked up a stone and followed him, dropping it into his hand. "Pretend it's a seed, OK?"

He looked up at Dot, and little by little his frown turned into a smile. "Thanks, Dot. All right, let's do it!"

They locked P.T. Flea in the circus wagon, then rode back to Ant Island. Flik and Dot rounded up the Blueberries and slowly climbed the tree where the mechanical bird was hidden. Meanwhile, the bugs gate-crashed a banquet where Hopper had made himself and the grasshoppers the guests of honor. At first he got mad, then he seemed to calm down. "I guess we could use a little entertainment."

Francis, Slim, and Heimlich did their clown act, and then Manny the magician took the stage. He put the Queen into a box and closed it. "And now: Insectus transformitus!" When Manny opened the box, Gypsy stepped out!

High in the tree, Flik sprang into action. "That's the signal!"

As Hopper spoke, Flik struggled to his feet. "You're wrong, Hopper. Ants are not meant to serve grasshoppers. I've seen these ants do great things. And year after year, they somehow manage to pick food for themselves and you. So, so, who is the weaker species? Ants don't serve grasshoppers. It's you who need us. We're a lot stronger than you say we are . . . and you know it, don't you?"

Then the most amazing thing happened. All the ants stood up to Hopper! As they closed in around him, he yelled.

"You ants get back!"

Atta flew up into his face. "You see, Hopper, nature has a certain order. The ants pick the food, the ants keep the food, and the grasshoppers leave!"

Thousands of ants charged, along with the circus bugs.

The grasshoppers were so scared that they ran off, leaving Hopper behind. "Come back here, you cowards! Don't leave!"

The ants shoved Hopper into the circus cannon and were about to shoot him off the island when the sky started to rumble. Suddenly, giant drops of water exploded all around them! Flik knew exactly what it was. "Rain!"

Seeing his chance to escape, Hopper grabbed Flik and flew into the tree. The circus bugs tried to rescue him but couldn't. Then Atta sneaked up from the other side. She snatched Flik away, and they raced off, with Hopper right behind them.

Dodging raindrops, Flik led Atta to the creek and hid her behind a rock. "I've got an idea! No matter what happens, stay down," said Flik.

Then he stood up and turned to face Hopper.

"No, please! Please, Hopper!" Flik cried.

Flik backed up into the brush, and Hopper caught him and started to choke him.

"You think it's over? I'll get more grasshoppers and be back next season, but you won't."

But Flik knew something that Hopper didn't. In the brush was a bird's nest. As a bird rose up over them, Hopper grinned. "Well, what's this? Another one of your little bird tricks?"

But it was no trick. The bird screeched, took Hopper in its beak, and fed him to her babies. "No, no, no, no! Aaaagh!"

Ant Island was safe again, thanks to Flik and the circus bugs. But the bugs were still performers, so when spring came they packed up the circus wagon. When they were finished, Atta called them over.

"I want to thank all of you for giving us back our hope, our dignity, and our lives."

Slim bowed, "And to you, Princess Atta. You have given us so much."

He joined the other bugs, including Francis, who was crying, and Heimlich, who had changed into a very fat butterfly. And off they rode.

Dot was sad to see them go. But things hadn't turned out too bad. After all, Flik was a hero. And Atta became the Queen.

Not bad for a bug's life!

Toy Secrets

Woody sits on my bed,
He's my favorite toy.
He ropes and wrangles,
For he's a darin' cowboy.

He's buddies with Buzz,
Who watches for danger.
With lots of cool gear,
For he's a real space ranger.

My Toys

The toys on the bed jump up and down,
Up and down, up and down.
The toys on the bed jump up and down,
All through the day.

The trains on their tracks go clickety-clack,
Clickety-clack, clickety-clack.
The trains on their tracks go clickety-clack,
All through the day.

The blocks in the box all build and tumble,
Build and tumble, build and tumble.
The blocks in the box all build and tumble,
All through the day.

The dolls on the shelf all laugh and play,
Laugh and play, laugh and play.
The dolls on the shelf all laugh and play,
All through the day.

Every kid loves toys. Take Andy, for instance. He's got Rex the dinosaur, Hamm the piggy bank, Mr. Potato Head, Slinky Dog, and dozens of others. But his favorite toy is Woody, a cowboy doll who talks when Andy pulls his string.

"Reach for the sky! This town ain't big enough for the two of us."
You probably like your toys, too. But did you ever wonder what
they do when you leave the room? At Andy's house, the toys come
alive!

One day, just before Andy's family was planning to move, Woody called the toys to order.

"Okay, first item today. Has everyone picked a moving buddy? I don't want any toys left behind. A moving buddy–if you don't have one, get one! Oh, yes, one minor note here. Andy's birthday party's been moved to today."

The toys gasped. The change of plans meant that today Andy would be getting new toys. And if Andy got new toys, he might throw his old ones away. Woody, sensing panic, tried to calm everyone down.

"I'm not worried. You shouldn't be worried," he said.

Then Hamm waddled up. "Birthday guests at three o'clock!"

At Woody's command, a group of toy soldiers hustled downstairs, carrying a baby monitor. Upstairs, the toys heard a soldier's voice through the speaker, describing Andy's presents. "The bow's coming off. We've got a lunchbox here. OK, second present . . . it appears to be . . . OK, it's bed sheets."

The toys seemed safe for another year. But there was one more surprise gift. "It's a huge package. Oh, wha–it's . . . it's–"

Rex bumped the speaker, and the batteries fell out. At the same time, there was a cheer from downstairs. The kids came racing upstairs to Andy's room as the toys scrambled back to their places.

Andy and his friends shoved Woody from his place on the bed and put a new toy there. They played with it, then raced back downstairs when it was time for games and prizes.

As the toys stirred, they heard a voice. "Buzz Lightyear to Star Command. Come in, Star Command. Why don't they answer?"

Woody climbed back up onto the bed and faced his worst fear: the coolest toy a kid could want, Buzz Lightyear.

He gulped. "There has been a bit of a mix-up. This is my spot, see, the bed here," Woody said to the new toy.

The other toys crowded around Buzz. Rex shook his hand. "Oh, I'm so glad you're not a dinosaur . . . Say! What's that button do?"

Buzz pressed the button, and wings popped out. All the toys were impressed–except for Woody. "These are plastic. He can't fly!"

"Yes, I can. Stand back, everyone. To infinity and beyond!"

Buzz leaped off the bed and headed straight for the floor. Then he bounced off a rubber ball and landed on a race car. The car took off on a track, spun through a loop, and bounced off a jump. Buzz flew out of the car, grabbing onto an airplane hung from the ceiling. After spinning around, he landed back on the bed. The toys cheered.

Woody couldn't believe it. "Well, in a couple of days, everything will be just the way it was. They'll see, I'm still Andy's favorite toy," he muttered.

Suddenly, the sound of barking interrupted the toys. They rushed to the window. It was Scud, the dog next door. With him was Sid, his owner, a kid who loved to torture toys.

Rex shook his head. "Oh, no. I can't bear to watch one of these again." As the toys looked on helplessly, Sid strapped a firecracker to his Combat Carl toy, lit the fuse, and blew the toy to smithereens.

Sid cheered. "Yes! He's gone! He's history. That was very sweet. Did you see that, Scud?"

Bo Peep turned away. "The sooner we move, the better."

Late that afternoon, the family finished packing boxes. Andy's mum told him they were going to Pizza Planet, his favorite restaurant, for the last time. She said he could bring one toy. Woody, who was listening, knew it would be either him or Buzz.

Seeing a space between the edge of the desk and the wall, Woody got an idea.

"Buzz . . . Buzz Lightyear, we've got trouble! A helpless toy—it's, it's trapped, Buzz!"

As Buzz leaned over the edge, Woody steered a remote control car toward him. Buzz dove out of the way, but the desk lamp swung around and accidentally knocked him out the window!

Mr. Potato Head saw it all. "Couldn't handle Buzz cutting in on your playtime, could you, Woody? Didn't want to face the fact that Buzz just might be Andy's new favorite toy, so you got rid of him."

"No! Wait! I can explain everything."

Woody never had the chance because just then Andy came into the room. "Mum, do you know where Buzz is?"

"Just grab some other toy. Now, come on."

"OK." Andy picked up Woody and carried him out to the van, past the bush where Buzz had landed. Buzz, seeing Andy take Woody into the van, raced after it and hopped on the back bumper.

The van pulled into a gas station and Andy got out, leaving Woody on the back seat. Woody looked up and saw Buzz, covered with mud, staring at him through the sunroof. "I just want you to know that even though you tried to terminate me, revenge is not an idea we promote on my planet."

Woody sighed with relief. "Oh. Oh, that's good."

"But we're not on my planet, are we?" Buzz lunged for Woody.

The two of them fell off the seat, out the open door, and rolled under the van. They were still on the ground, fighting, when the door slid shut and the van drove away.

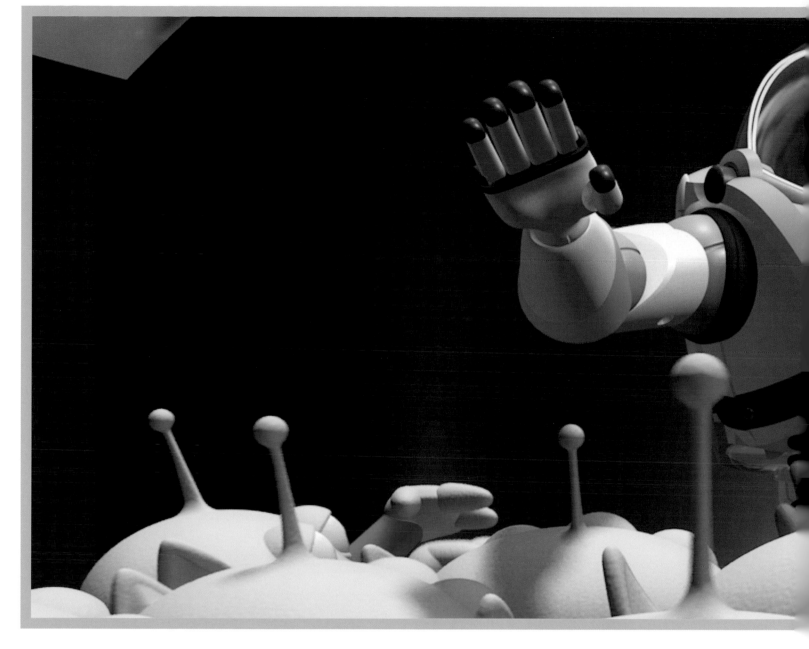

Woody watched the van leave. "I'm lost! Oh, I'm a lost toy."

Buzz was upset for a different reason. "And you, my friend, are responsible for delaying my rendezvous with Star Command."

"YOU-ARE-A-TOY! You aren't the real Buzz Lightyear; you're … you're an action figure. You are a CHILD'S PLAYTHING!"

Buzz shook his head. "You are a sad, strange little man, and you have my pity. Farewell."

As Buzz walked off, a Pizza Planet delivery truck with a plastic rocket on its roof pulled into the station. Woody had an idea. "Buzz! I found a spaceship!"

Buzz peered inside the truck.

"Now, you're sure this space freighter will return to its port of origin once it jettisons its food supply?"

Woody nodded. "Uh-huh. And when we get there, we'll be able to find a way to transport you home."

Sure enough, the truck took them to its port of origin–Pizza Planet. Buzz looked around in amazement. "What a spaceport!"

Then Woody spotted Andy with his mum and baby sister, Molly. Seeing a basket on Molly's stroller, Woody grinned. "OK, when I say go, we're going to jump in the basket." But Buzz was gone.

Buzz had spotted a game shaped like a rocket, and thought it might take him home. Inside, he found himself surrounded by squeeze-toy aliens.

"I am Buzz Lightyear. Who's in charge here?"

The aliens pointed up at a giant crane. "The claw is our master. The claw chooses who will go and who will stay. Shhhh! It moves."

Woody, who had followed Buzz into the game, gazed up in horror. "Oh, no! Sid!" Andy's cruel neighbor was at the controls.

The claw came down. It grabbed Buzz and pulled him upward. Woody clung to his legs, desperately trying to pull him free.

Sid was thrilled. "All right! Double prizes!"

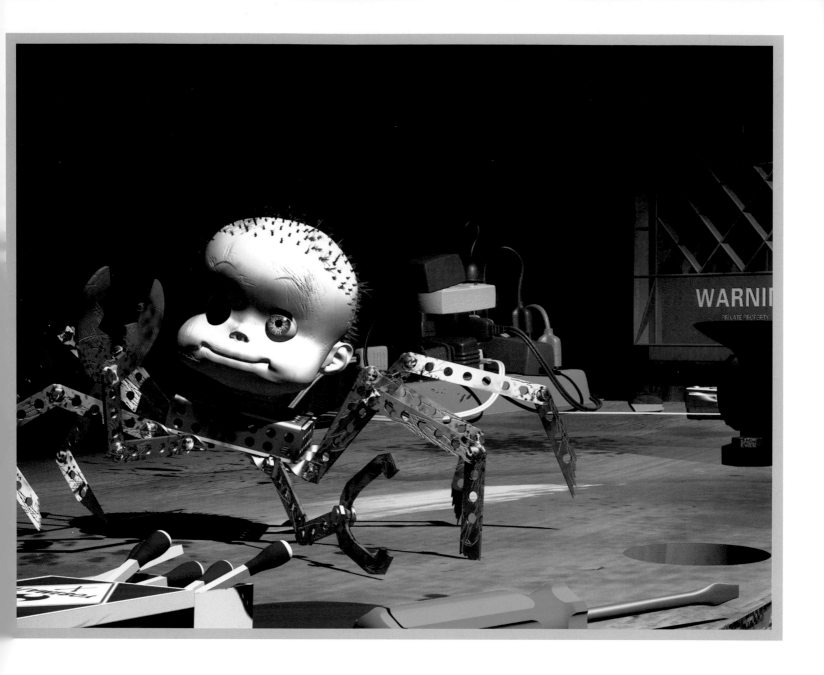

Sid raced home with Woody and Buzz in his backpack. He tossed the pack onto his bed, shut the door, and went downstairs.

Woody got out of the pack, ran across the bed, and leaped onto the doorknob. "Locked! There's got to be another way out of here."

There was a noise behind him, and a doll's head looked out from under the bed. Woody smiled. "Hi there, little fella. Come out here. Do you know a way out of here?"

The head continued toward him, propelled by a creepy, spider-like body made from the pieces of an Erector set. In horror, Woody scrambled back up onto the bed. "B-B-B-Buzz!"

The doll was joined by other mutant toys assembled from parts of different toys by Sid. Woody jumped inside the backpack and Buzz zipped it shut, punching a button on his chest. "Mayday! Mayday! Come in Star Command! Send reinforcements!"

He adjusted his laser light and turned to Woody.

"I've set my laser from stun to kill."

"Yeah, and if anyone attacks us we can blink 'em to death."

But instead of attacking, the mutant toys crept back out of sight. Woody and Buzz were safe . . . for the time being, at least.

The next morning, when Sid went downstairs, Woody jumped to his feet. "The door—it's open! We're free!"

He and Buzz raced for the hallway, but their path was blocked by the mutant toys. As the monsters approached, Buzz turned to Woody. "Shield your eyes!" He fired his laser. Nothing happened.

Woody shook his head in disgust. "Oh, you idiot—you're a TOY! Use your karate chop action!"

Woody pushed a button on Buzz's back and Buzz's arms began chopping. The mutant toys backed away, giving Woody and Buzz room to slip through the door.

While Woody was scouting the hallway, Buzz ducked inside another room. Behind him, a voice rang out. "Calling Buzz Lightyear. This is Star Command." The voice was coming from a commercial on TV, advertising Buzz Lightyear toys. Woody had been right after all.

Buzz was just a toy. Stunned, Buzz staggered to the top of the stairs. He opened his wings and jumped, hoping to fly. Instead, he crashed to the floor.

By the time Woody found him, Buzz had been discovered by Sid's sister, Hannah. She had dressed him up for a tea party and given him a new name. "Would you like some tea, Mrs. Nesbit?"

When Hannah left the room, Woody ran inside. He found Buzz with one arm. "Look at me. I can't even fly out of a window."

Woody smiled. "Out the window . . . Buzz, you're a genius!"

He dragged Buzz back into Sid's room, then stood in the window and called to the toys in Andy's room across the way. "Hey, guys! Guys! Hey!"

When the toys appeared, Buzz wouldn't help. So Woody picked up Buzz's arm and waved it, as if Buzz were standing behind the window frame. "Hiya, fellas. To infinity and beyond!"

But Woody held the arm too high, and Mr. Potato Head saw that it had been broken off. "Murderer! You murdering dog!"

Once again, the toys believed that Woody had done something awful to Buzz. As they hurried away from the window, Woody tried to stop them. "You've got to help us, please! You don't know what it's like over here!"

But it was no use. Before Woody could turn around, the mutants were all over Buzz.

Woody tried to stop them. "All right, back! Back, you cannibals!"

But the toys grabbed Buzz's arm and pushed Woody aside.

When they backed away, Buzz's arm was in place! Woody couldn't believe it. "Hey! Hey, they fixed you!" He tried to thank the mutant toys, but they scrambled back under the bed.

Sid came into the room with a brand-new rocket. "What am I going to blow? Man . . . hey, where's that wimpy cowboy doll?"

As Woody hid under a milk crate, Sid spotted Buzz. He set his tool box on the crate, trapping Woody. Then he picked up Buzz and taped the rocket to his back. "Yes! To infinity and beyond!"

There was a clap of thunder, and it started to rain. Sid looked outside. "Aw, man." He sat at the window, waiting for it to stop.

Sid wasn't the only one hoping for sunshine. Next door, Andy and his mum had finished packing for their move the next day.

Andy went to bed, sad that he never found his favorite toys.

   While Andy and Sid slept, Woody called to Buzz for help. Buzz lay with the rocket on his back, too sad to move. "I'm just a toy."

   Woody glared at him. "Look, over in that house is a kid who thinks you are the greatest and it's not because you're a space ranger, pal. It's because you're a toy. You are his toy!"

   A few moments later, the crate began to shake. Buzz was trying to push the tool box off! "Come on, sheriff. There's a kid over in that house who needs us. Now, let's get you out of this thing!"

   Just as Buzz managed to free Woody, Sid's alarm clock rang.

   Sid jumped out of bed, grabbed Buzz, and headed outside.

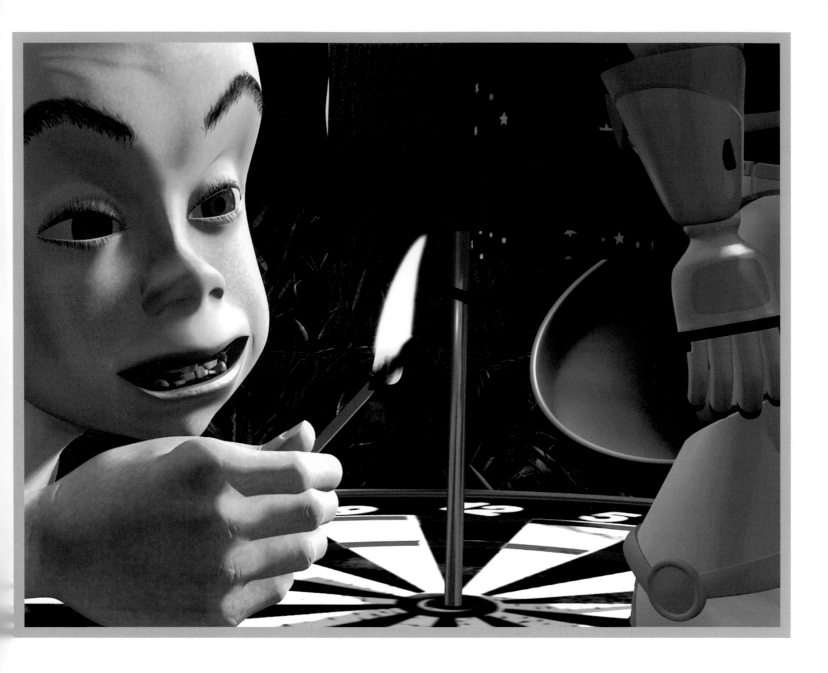

As Sid's toys crept out from under the bed, Woody asked them for help. "Please, he's my friend, he's the only one I've got." The toys gathered around. "OK, I think I know what to do, and if it works, it'll help everybody."

Working together, they escaped to the backyard, where Sid was starting to light the rocket. Suddenly he saw Woody lying nearby. "Hey! How'd you get out here?"

As Sid watched, an army of mutant toys rose from the grass and marched toward him. Woody grinned. "From now on, you must take good care of your toys. Because if you don't, we'll find out, Sid."

Sid ran screaming into the house.

As Woody rushed to help Buzz, a car horn honked. Next door, Andy's family and their moving truck were leaving. Buzz, with the rocket still strapped to his back, motioned to Woody. "Come on!"

They raced after the truck and grabbed onto the back. Woody held on, but Buzz fell to the street. "Buzz!"

Thinking fast, Woody found Andy's toy box inside the moving van and dug out the remote-controlled car. He tossed it into the street and steered it toward Buzz, who got on.

Mr. Potato Head, thinking Woody was trying to get rid of another toy, called to the others. "Get him! Toss him overboard!"

"No, no, wait!" But they pushed Woody into the street.

Woody bounced off the pavement and onto the car, right next to Buzz. They chased after the van in the remote-controlled car. But the batteries ran out, and it slowed to a stop.

Woody looked around. Seeing the sun through Buzz's helmet, he used it to focus sunlight on the rocket fuse. When the fuse lit, Woody grabbed Buzz, and they rocketed toward the moving truck, soaring in the air—but missed!

Buzz popped open his wings, tearing away the rocket from his back. The two of them glided over Andy's van towards Andy's mom's car. "Hey, Buzz! You're flying!"

They dipped through the sunroof and into an open box next to Andy. He let out a happy yell. "Hey! Wow! Woody! Buzz!"

A few months later, Woody, Buzz and the other toys were gathered around the baby monitor once again. It was their first Christmas in the new house, and Andy was opening his presents.

Woody smiled. "Buzz Lightyear, you're not worried, are you?"

"Me? No, no. Are you?"

"Now, Buzz, what could Andy possibly get that is worse than you?"

Woody and Buzz looked at each other. Downstairs, they heard Andy yell, "It's a puppy!"